An Order of Amelie, Hold the Fries

Nina Schindler

43

ANNICK PRESS

TORONTO + NEW YORK + VANCOUVER

Text © 2004 by Nina Schindler
Second Printing, September 2004

Annick Press Ltd.
All rights reserved. No part of this work covered by the copyrights hereon may be
reproduced or used in any form or by any means—graphic, electronic, or mechanical—
without the prior written permission of the publisher.

Original title: Fisch an Fahrrad
© 2003 by C.Bertelsmann Jugendbuch Verlag, a division of Verlagsgruppe Random
House GmbH, München, Germany

Translated by Rob Barrett
Edited by Pam Robertson
Designed by Irvin Cheung/iCheung Design
Copy-edit by Naomi Pauls

Cataloging in Publication

Schindler, Nina
    An order of Amelie, hold the fries / by Nina Schindler; translated by Robert
Barrett. -- North American ed.

Translation of: Fisch an Fahrrad.
ISBN 1-55037-861-9 (bound).--ISBN 1-55037-860-0 (pbk.)

I. Barrett, Robert (Robert James) II. Title.

PZ7.S357Or 2004   j833'.92   C2004-901123-5

The Publisher would like to thank Lisa Cheung, Jo-Ann Panneton, Jeane Treloar,
Doodles, Gino Burich, and Kathy Sigstad.

Printed and bound in Canada.

Published in the U.S.A. by   **Distributed in Canada by**   **Distributed in the U.S.A. by**
Annick Press (U.S.) Ltd.   Firefly Books Ltd.   Firefly Books (U.S.) Inc.
                                 66 Leek Crescent   P.O. Box 1338
                                 Richmond Hill, ON   Ellicott Station
                                 L4B 1H1   Buffalo, NY 14205

Visit our website at: **www.annickpress.com**

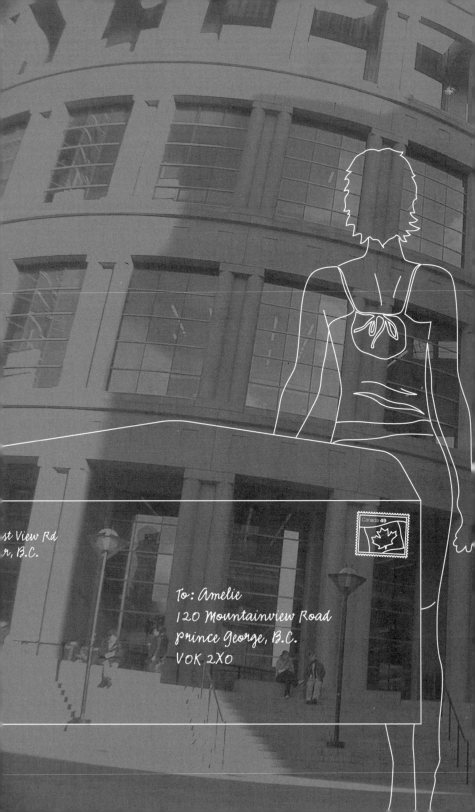

st View Rd
r, B.C.

Canada 49

To: Amelie
120 Mountainview Road
Prince George, B.C.
V0K 2X0

December 15th

Dear (as yet) unknown Amelie,
   I couldn't believe it. I was just walking behind you, admiring your long, beautiful legs, the perfect fit of your leather pants, your short blonde hair, and the confident way you carry yourself, when you dropped a piece of paper!
   Now, I've always thought stuff like that only happens in the movies—or maybe to other guys, but definitely not to me. So when I bent down and picked it up, I got a major shock. For lo and behold, there at the top were your name and address. Immediately I thought I must have gone completely mad. Crazy!!
   You may not know this, but I actually passed you earlier and thought you were somewhere between amazing and drop-dead gorgeous. After I got over being stunned, I turned around and started tailing you, because I just had to know more about you—this chick who runs around looking like a model. That I should be rewarded with your address, who would have thought?? I never would have dreamed it! Now I'm floating in 7th heaven.
   What can I say? I'm an incurable romantic.
   Allow me to introduce myself . . .
   But wait. Perhaps you did notice me before you passed your address on to me—???? If so, you

already know that I'm kind of lanky and 6 feet tall (actually, 5'11?", but maybe what's left is still to come . . .). I sometimes wear glasses (really, only when I'm driving) and I'm in Grade 12. That's why we met where we did. I was just on my way to the public library to check out books by this writer I'm supposed to do a paper on. In a state of temporary insanity, even though I like his music and poetry, I foolishly picked Leonard Cohen. But there's just so much to cover!

I have no idea where to start telling you about myself. I'm almost 17 and I live at home, have a younger sister (a pain), and am looking for someone I can laugh with and talk to, go out with or go nowhere with. Someone who's not afraid to do whatever comes to mind. (Would it put you off if I told you that doing "whatever comes to mind" is at least as important as the rest? I hope not. You look like a girl who's adventurous and not afraid of a good time. That's what made me dare to write you in the first place.)

So, when I picked up that piece of paper, all of a sudden I had this weird hope that you might be the right kind of woman for me.

What do you think?

Is there a chance for us?

If there is, that would be so cool.

Expectant, yet anxious, I look forward to your reply, hoping your answer is positive.

Tim

SELECTED POEMS 1956 – 1968

LEONARD COHEN

...red to be a minor poe...ca... in his career, ...me on... of the m... ...t and popula... ...ters of ...1960s... ...duce an ext... ...ody of... ...n in Montreal... ...interest in ...erature from a... ...ort of p... ...in *Spice Box of Earth*; brou... ...ribution... ...60s; he had ...fa... ...st seven yea... ...Cohen... novels, and ...first album, ...Suzanne" and... ...publication of his novel *Beautiful Los*... Ja... Joyce is not dead: He is living ...mic... Cohen." Leonard Cohen would co...

120 Mountainview Road,
Prince George, B.C.
V0K 2X0
E-mail: amarchand@webmail.bc

Dear Tim,

I'm afraid to say we won't be seeing each other again, simply because we've never met.

Honest! Before you collapse in despair, just finish reading.

Sorry to have to say this, but I'm not the person you think I am. I'm not the kind of girl you would ever have tailed. I'm tall and boring and have long, dark hair and don't carry myself in any way that someone might call confident.

Besides, if we passed on the street, I doubt you would ever see my hair anyway, since I prefer to keep it in curlers most of the time—big, pink ones—and always have my head covered in at least two scarves. I wouldn't be caught dead in leather pants. I much prefer baggy sweats (they're my all-time fave . . . and so very practical—they hide my big fat fanny).

And to top it all off, I'm not available. I'm as good as engaged.

The solution to this riddle is quite simple and won't be reason enough for a trip to seventh or tenth or whatever heaven. A girlfriend of mine from work, Vanessa, and I are both on an interim break right now and away on vacation. She wanted me to read some book, so I gave her my address here (at my parents') so she could send it to me.

She obviously lost my address before she even left town, so I guess I might as well give up waiting for that package . . .

Unfortunately, I'm not at liberty to give you her contact info (protection of privacy, you understand). I'm not even certain where she went for vacation anyhow, and she'll be gone for ages. Even if you manage to track Vanessa down and still wanna try your luck, you'll have to deal with her boyfriend, some kind of tae kwon do master. So beware.

Take care and good luck with your paper.

Amelie

Delete Reply Reply All Forward Print

From: amarchand@webmail.bc
To: nessacontessa@webmail.bc
Subject: How could you!?!

Dear Nessa,

How can you be such a flake?

If tossing my note to the four winds is how you take care of a friend's address, I'll never get that book! Fortunately, Leah in Personnel found your parents' address in your file. I thought I'd quickly write you before you take off on your fabulous Hawaiian vacation.

Just my luck, my address fell into the hands of some pimply-faced teenager (at least, he sounds like one), who thought it was yours and sent you a pickup letter. Actually, it was quite original, kind of charming, but unfortunately, it was addressed to me.

So I guess you'll be missing out on an admirer. Not that it matters much, given the hordes that are already tripping after you.

The strange thing is, the guy mentioned liking Leonard Cohen. And the fact he's one of my favorite writers, and you were about to send me "The Spice Box of Earth," is too much.

What a weird coincidence!

I'll be hanging around my parents' place for another 10 days, spending a bit more time with Bastian, etc., then it's back to the hotel grind, while you enjoy the sunny beaches of Waikiki. I can't believe you got so much more time off.

There is no justice . . .

Say hi to Justin for me and be sure to get all the rest you can—the next six months are going to be killer. Sometimes I seriously wonder why I was so determined to go into hotel management. Maybe it was those high-flying dreams of palatial white hotels in the Caribbean, rubbing elbows with the rich and the beautiful under the palm trees . . . and hardly ever doing an ounce of work.

What a joke! My only contact with the rich and beautiful is trying to jam all their fancy luggage into the elevators, and sometimes getting stuck between floors as a reward. But, of course, that never happens at our noble Royal Pacific Hotel!!

Take care and have an awesome time,

Amelie

Dear Amelie,

I opened your letter with a lump in my throat, read it with trembling hands, and folded it up with tears in my eyes.

Tears of laughter.

It's the kind of thing that could only happen to me.

There, right in front of me, is the woman of my dreams, and she's already promised to someone else. Oh, cruel fate. And to top it all off, she isn't even the one I thought, but someone else altogether . . .

But since everything seemed to be a daydream anyway, just a trip to fantasyland, I'm not really heartbroken. Thanks, in no small part, to your letter.

I'm a serious devotee of curlers and baggy sweatpants—I find them exceptionally sexy. What a shame that they get branded as unflattering and boring. Anybody with an ounce of aesthetic refinement knows that curlers truly bring out women's beauty. I'm especially fond of those neon-pink ones— what sass and flair!—although lots can be said in favor of such classic tones as pale green or simple white. All of which enhance the natural shine of a woman's hair a great deal, and should be celebrated as the modern miracles they are. (As you can see, I may be a victim of too many commercials. . . . They've certainly left their indelible mark.)

I wish I could carry on discussing the merits of curlers, but unfortunately I have a ton of homework to do. I still have a lot of Cohen to read. Up until now, I had read only a few of his poems ("You Do Not Have to Love Me" is my favorite so far), but this report has me flying through them all. I had no idea that he had written so many. I should have picked some poet who died young and left only one slim volume. That would have been so much easier.

Most likely I've screwed myself royally by admitting all of this to you. Now you must think I'm lazy and ignorant, as well as illiterate. But it's not true! Honestly. If you can believe it (it's surely a stretch), I've collected—and even read!—the complete volumes of Spider-Man from start to finish. An absolute fact!

Oh, the cultural high ground. But alas, I've now got to return to my books. Everything about Cohen needs to be researched: his biography, his poems, his friends, his enemies, his critics. My head is a whirlwind of dates and bibliographies, with a musical soundtrack. Information overload! I'm going to explode!

Please, please write me again and make me laugh!

Show some support for our country's academic future.

Tim

E · Wednesday, February 04, 2004 A35
Tim...
DEAR AGNES
Dear Agnes: I need your help. My son is 17 years old and plans to drop out of high school even though his marks are quite high. He says school is boring and he just wants to make his own money. All my arguments fall on deaf ears. How can I convince him to stay in school?
— Concerned Mother
Give him a complete set of Spider-Man comics.

From: tim@yipee.ca
To: amarchand@webmail.bc
Subject: ouch!

Amelie,

What a low blow!

My teachers run me ragged, trying to jam more and more crap into my already tired and overworked brain. I study like crazy, tearing my hair out, and not one word of encouragement from you!

Exhausted and disappointed,

Tim

Encouragement.

加油！加油！

THE GREAT CHINESE POSTCARD COMPANY

archand
untainview Road,
George, B.C.
K 2X0

Thanks for the comfort...

Why in the world
are you spending so long
in Prince George?

Hawaii

The Islands of Aloha!

Dear Amelie,

It's wonderful here. I want to stay forever. Justin is already jealous, because of all the surfers who flirt with me down at the beach. It's kind of cute—for now.

Don't let work get you down. Just remember our plans. One day we'll make it to Barbados (or was it Tobago?).

Cheers,

Nessa (tanned and wild for adventure)

Amelie Marchand
120 Mountainview
Prince George, B.C.
V0K 2X0   Canada

Aloha. Mention the word and a thousand dreamy images spring to mind. What could be more romantic than a full moon through palm fronds?

Picture of an Unknown Woman

Who are you? What do you do?
So you live in Vancouver?
When are you coming back?

ROYAL PACIFIC
HOTEL

Registration Form

THE ROYAL PACIFIC HOTEL
1518 Grand Avenue
Vancouver, B.C.
V1X 8G5 Canada

NAME

TITLE

OMPANY

ME ADDRESS

./MAIL CODE

S TELEPHONE

NUMBER

'E

ATE

I'm a hotel management trainee and way too old for you. I got back to Vancouver this morning and am working 24/7.

Bye. It's been fun, but I don't have any time.

Good luck with school,

A.

FIC HOTEL
e or double. Please apply 14.5% tax to the above rate.
nust be guaranteed with a 1-night deposit.
t be cancelled before 6:00 p.m. on the arrival date.

ROYAL PACIFIC HOTEL

Cruel, hard-hearted, egotistical former pen "pal,"

How can you be so cold and just drop me like that???

Please don't rip asunder this delicate web I have spun with so much devotion. Even an important, busy management trainee such as yourself should be able to spare a minute or two to write the occasional short note.

These last few weeks have been exhausting and were only bearable because of your correspondence. Whenever something arrived from you, my heart beat like mad. When nothing came, I was sick with disappointment. Devastated. Only writing to you has made my life worthwhile. And this is how it should end??????????????

NO! NO! NO! NO! NO! NO! NO! NO! NO! NO!

Is it because you're "as good as engaged"? What would an almost-fiancé have against a few innocent little notes?

I admit that I'm envious of this mystery man. Green with envy, to be exact. Who is this guy hiding in the background, anyway?

Of course, you don't have to answer that. I would be happy even if you just said boo.

Please, please, pretty please, don't leave me like this. Make my days exciting again with your nasty, stinging notes.

In breathless anticipation . . . with my head still spinning from math, chemistry, and irregular French verbs, I await a sign of life,

Tim

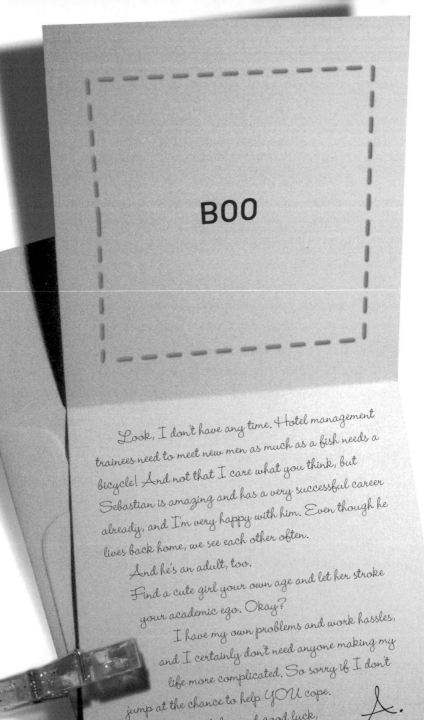

BOO

Look, I don't have any time. Hotel management trainees need to meet new men as much as a fish needs a bicycle! And not that I care what you think, but Sebastian is amazing and has a very successful career already, and I'm very happy with him. Even though he lives back home, we see each other often.

And he's an adult, too.

Find a cute girl your own age and let her stroke your academic ego. Okay?

I have my own problems and work hassles, and I certainly don't need anyone making my life more complicated. So sorry if I don't jump at the chance to help YOU cope.

Again, good-bye and good luck,

A.

I never knew that riding a bicycle
could be so much fun.

See!!

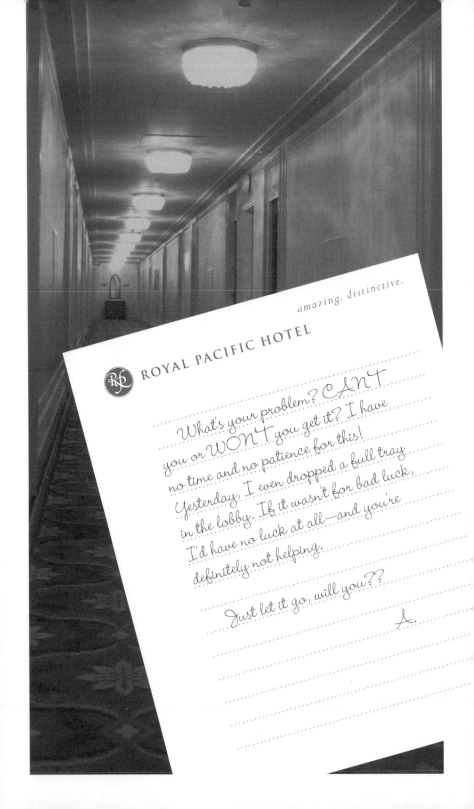

ROYAL PACIFIC HOTEL

amazing. distinctive.

What's your problem? CAN'T
you or WON'T you get it? I have
no time and no patience for this!
Yesterday, I even dropped a full tray
in the lobby. If it wasn't for bad luck,
I'd have no luck at all—and you're
definitely not helping.

Just let it go, will you??

A.

Boy, have you BLOWN it!!!
BALLOON MADNE
Vancouver's Largest Supplier of Novelty Balloons
Thanks for trying, but
WRONG!!!
Boy, have you
BLOWN it!!!
NICE is an insult.
It's gotta be the dullest, stupidest,
most meaningless word in the
English language.
Good-bye! I mean it!!!
A.

This is to make up for my using such a stupid word—a momentary lapse on my part, when I surely meant to write something much more poetic . . . Consider this an invitation to watch Grand Hotel starring Greta Garbo at the Rialto on February 10th at 7 p.m.

See you then,
Tim the Persistent

The Rialto Theatre
GRAND HOTEL
Showing At 19:00
Tues 02.10.04
Screen   Row   Seat
General Admission
9.00
ADULT
20907679

GRAND HOTEL
ADULT   9.00
Screen Row Seat
Gen. Admiss
02.10.04
19.00
20907679

GRAND HOTEL
19:00
02.10.04
Screen   Row   Seat
General Admission

GRAND HOTEL
ADULT   9.00
Screen Row Seat
Gen. Admiss
02.10.04
19.00
20907680

ROYAL PACIFIC HOTEL

Work Schedule

Thanks, but no thanks,
I don't have the time. Besides,
I've already seen the movie.
As I said, find some other girl.

Ciao, ~~Amelie~~ Amelie

EMPLOYEE: Amelie

TIME / WEEK	MON	TUE	WED	THURS	FRI	SAT	SUN
				X			
7:00	X			X			
8:00	X			X			
9:00	X	X	X	X		X	
10:00	X	X	X		X	X	
11:00	X	X	X	X	X	X	
12:00	X		X	X	X		X
13:00	X	X	X	X	X	X	X
14:00		X	X	X	X	X	X
15:00		X	X	X	X	X	X
16:00		X	X		X	X	X
17:00		X	X		X	X	X
18:00		X					

Longee Noodle Palace

正麵館

288 West 8th Avenue, Vancouver, BC, V5Y 1N5
Tel: (604) 555-0384, Fax: (604) 555-2872

Licensed Premise • Authentic Atmosphere

Went to the movie by myself. Now I'm bummed because I don't have anyone to talk to about it.

There is no other girl, and really, who else would have appreciated such a film but you? I failed my math test and I'm in desperate need of moral support, preferably from a future hotel manager. Not even eating an entire order of Egg Foo Yung has helped.

T.

- Free delivery on orders over $15.
- Extra MSG upon request!
- Customized menus & moderately priced catering for bar mitzvahs, weddings and birthday parties...

Monday to Saturday 8:00 am to 1:00 am
Sunday 10:00 am to 10:00 pm

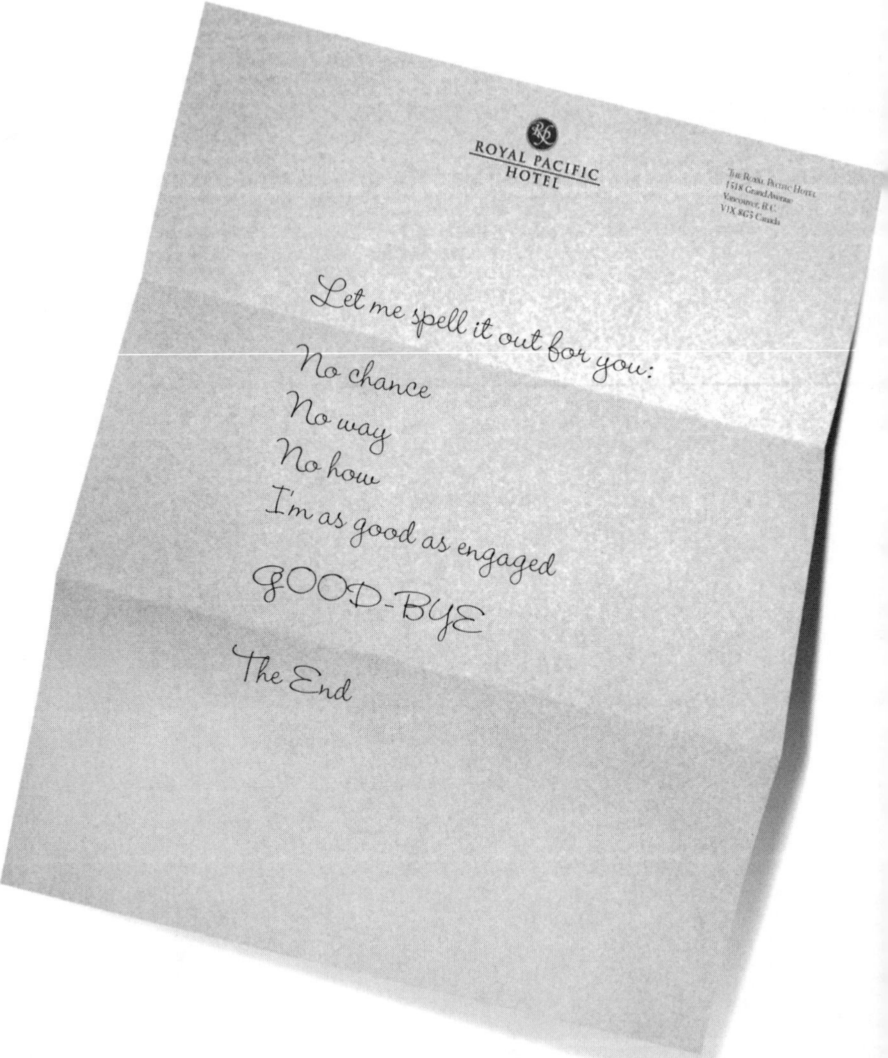

ROYAL PACIFIC
HOTEL

The Royal Pacific Hotel
1516 Grand Avenue
Vancouver, B.C.
V7X 8G5 Canada

Let me spell it out for you:

No chance

No way

No how

I'm as good as engaged

GOOD-BYE

The End

From: tim@yipee.ca

To: amarchand@webmail.bc

Subject: Curious

I was so distraught yesterday that I had to see what you look like.
Were you the plump, dark-haired girl with buck teeth and NO engagement
ring? That uniform doesn't do a thing for you!

No offence.

A friend, who means well if you would just let him.

From: amarchand@webmail.bc
To: tim@yipee.ca
Subject: Unbelievable

Were you the scrawny loser sitting on the couch in the lobby for hours, gawking? Where do you get your clothes? Sally Ann?

Give it up. Alright?

A.

From: amarchand@webmail.bc
To: sebastian@hotpost.com
Subject: Next weekend

Dear Sebastian,

Reception told me you called. I'm really sorry I missed you. Right now, I'm doing room service. Working dawn to midnight, I can't tell whether I'm coming or going. Still, I check my e-mail fairly often, so it's better if you drop me a line rather than give me a call. Everything goes through reception and they have a hard time tracking people down, so getting private calls during work hours is frowned upon. I'm not even allowed to have my cell on.

Every day, I meet the weirdest people. Yesterday, some guy gave me a $10 tip just for making his bed. Last Thursday, as I was cleaning the bathroom in the presidential suite, a guest walked in—buck naked! I couldn't tell who was more freaked out, me or him. I murmured some excuse about needing more towels and fled, almost knocking down the barely dressed woman close behind him. It was like a scene straight out of the movies.

My boss looks like she chews sour cherries all day but is actually quite nice, if you follow her orders to a T. She even praised me a few days back when I told her that one of our guests had swiped a terrycloth robe—in just enough time to get it onto his bill. You'd think rich people wouldn't stoop that low, but somehow they just assume it's part of the service.

Well, it's already 11 and I've gotta be up at 6.

Sleep well,
Amelie
XOXOXOX

P.S. Sorry, but next weekend I'm on duty.
Maybe the following weekend . . .

Celebrate Valentine's Day in a fitting manner. Grant yourself the pleasure of a purely platonic walk through Stanley Park.

(Please say yes. I would like to apologize in person for my stupid jab about wearing a uniform. I'm sure that even if you do have one you look lovely in it.)

amazing. distinctive.

ROYAL PACIFIC HOTEL

There's just no shaking you, is there??

Jeez...
    Well, I don't enjoy going for walks
at all—especially when it's freezing outside.
However, I guess I could accept an
invitation to a movie instead. But no
crummy little hole with only 20 seats, like
the Rialto. And absolutely NO popcorn.
    Dead on my feet,

                                Amelie

THE ROYAL PACIFIC HOTEL | 1518 Grand Avenue, Vancouver, B.C. , V1X 8G5 Canada

From: tim@yipee.ca

To: amarchand@webmail.bc

Subject: Hooray! She comes!

How about a suitably sappy flick? (NO popcorn, of course.) The Alma Theatre is screening classic romances all through the weekend.

On Friday they're showing An Affair to Remember, Saturday it's Breakfast at Tiffany's, and Sunday they have Casablanca.

Which one do you want to see?

How will I recognize you?

I still don't know what you look like!

I can't approach every long-haired woman not wearing leather pants. Maybe it'd be best if you did come in a baggy track suit and curlers.

Can't wait,

Tim

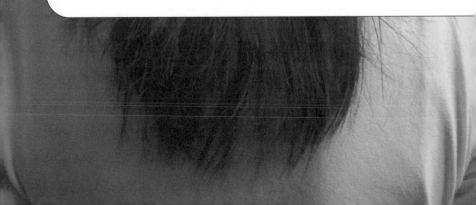

From: amarchand@webmail.bc
To: tim@yipee.ca
Subject: Vital statistics

I'll take Breakfast at Tiffany's, because I have Saturday off. I'm 6'6" (just kidding, 5'11" without shoes) and I have long, dark brown hair. Sorry, but no buck teeth.

How will I recognize you?

A.

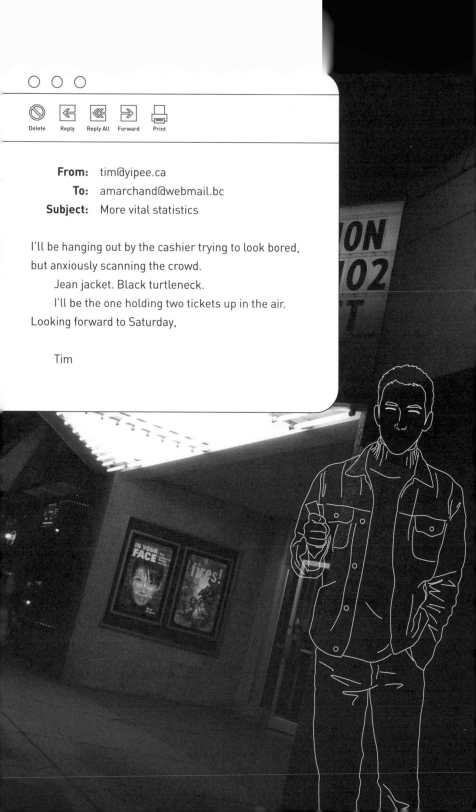

From: tim@yipee.ca
To: amarchand@webmail.bc
Subject: More vital statistics

I'll be hanging out by the cashier trying to look bored, but anxiously scanning the crowd.

Jean jacket. Black turtleneck.

I'll be the one holding two tickets up in the air.
Looking forward to Saturday,

Tim

From: sebastian@hotpost.com

To: amarchand@webmail.bc

Subject: Great news!

Dear Amelie,

Thanks a lot for the e-mail. Good to hear that you're still alive.

I love hearing about the stuff you do during the day. But you sound so tired! Are you sure you're not overdoing it?

I have to admit that I'm quite worried about you. You sound really stressed out and your e-mails have become so impersonal.

It's time I came to take care of you, hon.

I'll try to organize my schedule so that I can come to Vancouver in the near future. I've got some really great news to tell you. (At the moment, everything is top secret.) Soon I'll be able to give you all the details—and boy, will you be surprised! Everything is going to be different, and finally we'll be together.

How does that sound?

I'll be able to tell you more soon.

Love,
Sebastian

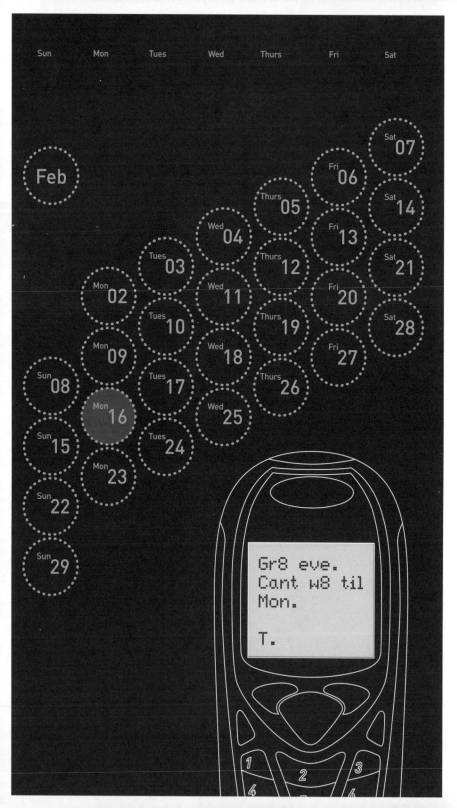

From: sebastian@hotpost.com
To: amarchand@webmail.bc
Subject: Monday

Dear Amelie,

The time has come. Please take Monday night off—I'm coming to Vancouver! It's very important! I've got wonderful news! I can't wait to tell you everything. Get ready for some changes!

Love,
Sebastian

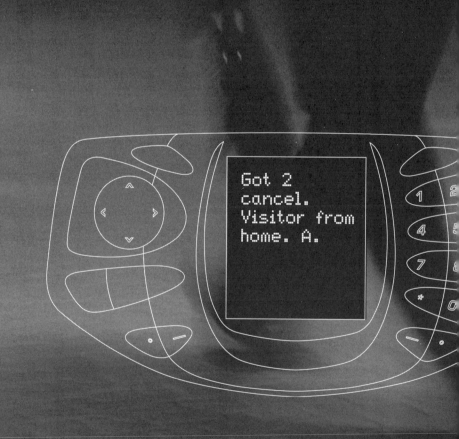

From: tim@yipee.ca
To: amarchand@webmail.bc
Subject: Roger. Message received. Over and out.

Saw you by accident in Stanley Park, with a guy I assume is your fiancé. Thought you hated walks??

I'm expendable, of course.

Life sucks.

You want efficiency and effec-
ness! You're tired of all the
s. In fact, you can't take it anoth-
day. (Never forget your envi-
ment affects you more than any
ther sign.) Eek! Is that mould?

Scorpio (Oct. 23 - Nov. 21)
Your relationships with
other people are
influenced by Mars.
Be careful! But there
is no reason to despair not — everything is as it seems.

ime
een
hat's
denly
You're
t's wise
ings you
you have
owing the

une 20)
n definitely
to be in the
eye more than
n the next sev-
ur dry cleaning.)
ght be involved
your boss more
u'll probably be
increased respon-
mething. Say yes.
une 21 - July 22)
A desire to get away
from it all is starting
to build up within you
now. That's because
ed a change of scenery!
with white sands,
and great room
in publish-
also

Read Leonard Cohen's

THE
FAVORITE
GAME

—there are always different
ways of looking at things.

Omnitel C&IS
Suite 105
20500 Production Way Tel 1+416 555 0465
Toronto, Ontario   Fax 1+416 555 6535
M3N 6T5 Canada   Web www.omnitelcis.com

omniitel COMMUNICATIONS & INFORMATION SYSTEMS

Dear Amelie,

I tried for hours to get a hold of you, but in that huge hotel of yours, not one person was able to track you down.

Now I'm sitting on a plane to Toronto, writing you a quick letter.

What's going on? We had a really nice time the other night, but you never gave me a definite answer. Just choose a day! What's holding you back?

I was under the impression that everything between us was clear and understood. Yet all of a sudden you come up with some feeble excuses. My parents want to have a date, and I have to book any time off well in advance. And if they transfer me, holidays will be very hard to come by.

I always thought you wanted a June wedding. I've done my best to make that possible—and now you don't seem to be into it.

Instead, you're acting distant. And that's not like you at all.

What's the problem? Aren't you happy?

This is THE chance for us! Every time I think about how this will change our lives I'm ecstatic.

I'll call you sometime in the next few days and I hope by then you'll have an answer for me.

Love,
Sebastian

Dear Amelie,

You must think me quite the idiot.
I certainly consider myself one. An evening of fun at the movies is definitely no reason to start playing the jealous lover. Please accept my heartfelt apologies and this bouquet of flowers—straight out of my neighbor's garden. (I asked permission first.) I was stupid. It won't happen again if you give me another chance.

I read The Favorite Game and agree with you that it's wonderful, very powerful—but there's no happy ending.

I LOVE happy endings.

Your not particularly happy Tim

From: amarchand@webmail.bc

To: tim@yipee.ca

Subject: Sigh

Oh Tim, you big goof,

The flowers smell like spring. They're perfect because I'm very confused right now. Who'll go out with me on Wednesday night and not talk about stupid things like feelings?

I need a break.

And chocolate chip cookies.

And someone who'll make me laugh.

Do you think you can manage that?

Amelie

Delete   Reply   Reply All   Forward   Print

From: tim@yipee.ca
To: amarchand@webmail.bc
Subject: Night out

Hey, at heart, I'm just an insensitive goon, but I try not to show it. So you can be certain that come Wednesday I'll only talk about hockey, cars, and the latest computer viruses. Promise. Is that insensitive enough?

My latest part-time grunt work has left me with enough dough for at least two almond mocha lattes and some cookies.

I'm looking forward to Wednesday.

Timmy the Tulip, the insensitive, muscle-brained goon

P.S. Who's going to get the next latte?

From: amarchand@webmail.bc

To: nessacontessa@webmail.bc

Subject: Got back

Dear Nessa,

I'm counting the days until you get here. You've been away far too long. I'm totally confused and need your smart-alecky remarks about life in general—and my problems in particular.

I did tell you about the guy who found my address, didn't I? Well, in the meantime, I've actually met the guy and he's really quite sweet—creative and funny. I don't think I've been bored one second, he makes me laugh so much. It's amazing, since technically he's still just a boy. (He's two years younger than me.)

So far, everything has been very innocent. We've gone to the movies a couple of times and for walks. It's really done wonders for me. Especially since Bastian is putting a lot of pressure on me right now. His company wants to transfer him to Chicago and, being Sebastian, he insists on getting married first. He has this picture in his head of me as his perfect accessory wife, decorating his home and going to cocktail parties with him. But that would mean I'd have to quit my training program—and he thinks that's no big deal!!! All of a sudden, he says he wants to get married really soon and that I've always talked about a June wedding. Not true! And June's only four months from now!

I'm not ready for that. My head starts spinning just thinking about it. Settling down? Once and for all? Besides, I love my (our) job, despite all my moaning and groaning. I want to finish my training and get some work experience—perhaps as the boss at the Ritz . . .

I'm bummed and I feel trapped.

What am I going to do?

Please get back soon so you can take care of your quite unhappy,

Amelie

Whom or what do you mean? Oeuvre or auth[or]

I would like to conclude my report by saying that before I started all the research about Cohen for this paper I had no idea about his variety and depth. Leonard Cohen is not only a very (passionate) musician and poet, but a masterful experimental novelist who has both delved into the social issues of his day and devoted himself to exploring the spiritual state of mankind? The seeming lightness cannot hide the fact that even in his (passionate) love poems there is a lot of substance to be found beneath the surface.

Repetition

Not politically correct; only male form used

Example!

I have learned to fully appreciate Cohen and his works during these weeks of research and know now that I will definitely return to his writing for further perusal. *Peruse? Not read?*

A precise report, without any doubt the result of extensive reading. Some expressions are too colloquial (slang) but overall an excellent work.

(A)

Out again?
Chinese
food?
Sweet N
sour
lap dog?
8 PM?

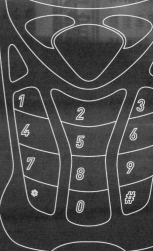

Cant w8!
Hope Seb
doesnt get
in the way.
Would B my
death. T.

Happiness is doubled
if shared by two.

Tried and true!

You better
believe it!

Omnitel C&IS
Suite 105
20500 Production Way   Tel   1+416 555 0465
Toronto, Ontario   Fax   1+416 555 6535
M3N 6T5 Canada   Web   www.omnitelcis.com

omniitel COMMUNICATIONS & INFORMATION SYSTEMS

Dear Amelie,

Your phone call yesterday has got me so worked up, I can't concentrate. So before I throw my laptop against the wall, I decided I should write you a letter and voice my anger. I tried calling you late last night, but your cell was off and I didn't feel like screaming into your mailbox.

What do you mean, you need more time to decide? Don't you know what you want anymore?

I, for one, am at a loss.

How am I supposed to interpret everything you said yesterday? Do you really want to call off the wedding? Right, right, we never made a big deal about being engaged, it was never official, that's true, but we did agree that we wanted to be together—or do I have that wrong now? Have you been misleading me? Have these last two years meant nothing to you? Haven't you been dreaming of a future together? Or was that just me? The world doesn't make sense anymore.

I don't know how I'll be able to explain your indecisiveness to my parents. I don't want them to think ill of you. I'll try to stall them for a while.

I'm hoping for clarification, and perhaps a loving word from you.

Love,

Sebastian

Meet
tonight?
Have off.
RSVP

jectives. In th... e d...
roximate a function near som...
dent should be able

- to visualize the tangent lin...
  and
- to determine on what inter...

dules:

Problem. Let f be a fun...
of f, g(x) = m (x - a) + f...
We know that the tange...
problem that we want to...
approximation to f. Mor...
determine for what x ne...

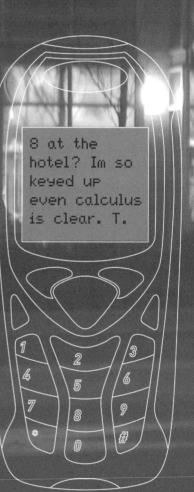

8 at the
hotel? Im so
keyed up
even calculus
is clear. T.

- Discussion [Using Flash]

- A LiveMath notebook th...

- A JavaScript module tha...
  problem

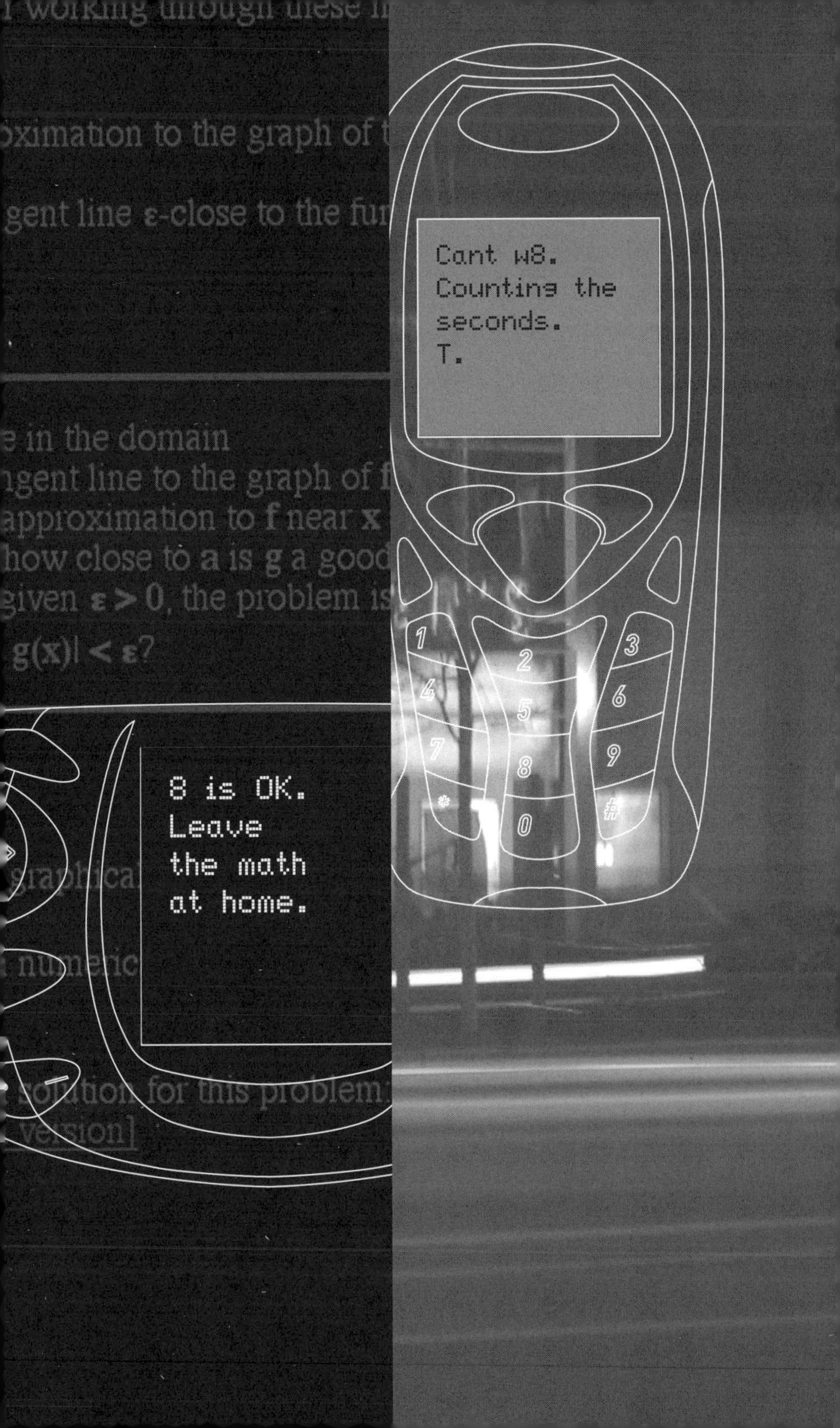

f working through these in

oximation to the graph of t

gent line ε-close to the fu

e in the domain
ngent line to the graph of f
approximation to f near x
how close to a is g a good
given $\varepsilon > 0$, the problem is

$g(x)| < \varepsilon$?

Cant w8.
Counting the
seconds.
T.

8 is OK.
Leave
the math
at home.

graphica

numeric

solution for this problem
version]

There once was a girl from Vancouver
Who was resistant to every maneuver
But finally the fireworks went off
And she pulled out all the stops
Embracing the boy who had wooed her

There once was a girl by the Fraser
Who met a boy who crazed her
He lured her with Cohen
And without them knowing
In the end all his charm would save her

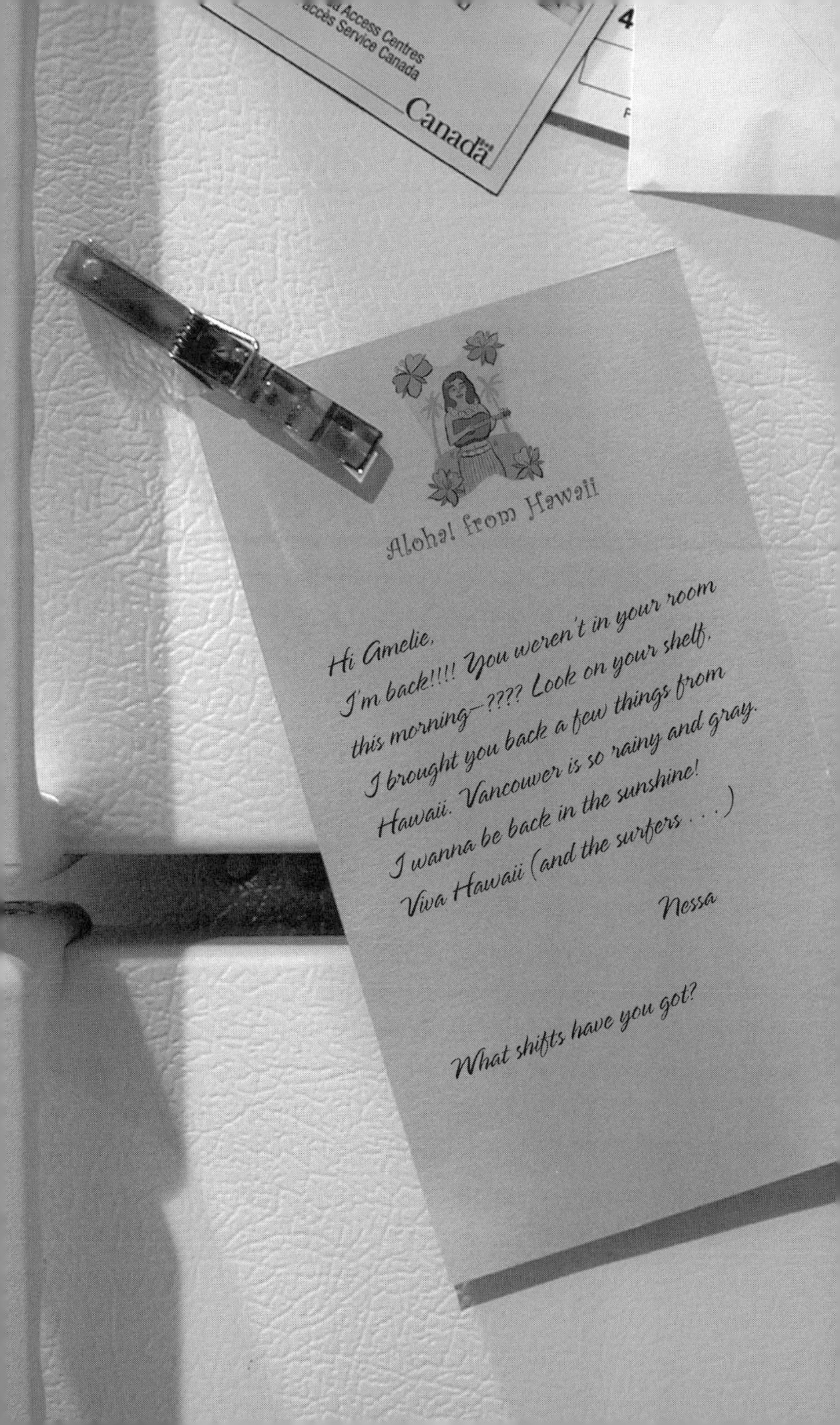

Aloha! from Hawaii

Hi Amelie,

I'm back!!!! You weren't in your room this morning—???? Look on your shelf, I brought you back a few things from Hawaii. Vancouver is so rainy and gray. I wanna be back in the sunshine! Viva Hawaii (and the surfers . . .)

Nessa

What shifts have you got?

Dearest Amelie,

Hard to believe that I'm actually back in school, sitting in history class. Brooks, my teacher, is doubtful I'm actually taking notes. But I just had to write to you. Otherwise, I might explode! I'm so happy I could sing (even all the major dates in history, in C-sharp). I'm in bliss. What an old-fashioned word, but there is no other way to express how I feel—I'm floating! On cloud 9. Or in 7th heaven. (I'll let someone else argue about which level.) I'm closing my eyes (not for long, otherwise Brooks might catch on), and I feel your lips on my lips, your hair tickles my face, and your hand seeks mine . . . I never thought love could be so great. Got to stop here because Brooks is getting suspicious.

Later, at home.
I'm sitting in my room (which you now know), and I look around and wish you were here. You are the most wonderful thing that has ever happened to me, and the most wonderful woman I've ever seen. No one has ever made me this happy. I could laugh and cry and rant like an idiot all day, screaming your name until my voice cracks. You have the most beautiful name, and I'm convinced that fate has brought us together. We were meant to be! No doubt! Amelie, I still can't believe it. But it's true, isn't it? You and I, us two, it really is happening.

Every hour, every minute, every second I don't see, hear, and kiss you is like an eternity.

Tim

Do you know what the craziest part is? I'm so deliriously happy that I'm going to do math now, voluntarily. Isn't that weird? But since I failed that test, I have to do my best on the makeup.

I'm missing you, counting the minutes until I can once more

hear your laugh
touch your face
and kiss your lips.

Tim

Hi Amelie,

I'm on restaurant duty and have to work 'til midnight. We'll have to talk later. Hawaii was great, but Jealous Justin was a real pain. So I got rid of him. Freedom!

Nessa, footloose and fancy-free

Everyone Gets Leied

From: amarchand@webmail.bc
To: tim@yipee.ca
Subject: Can't make it

Dear Tim,

I can't get away today. Two of my co-workers called in sick and I have to cover.

Sorry.

See you soon,

A.

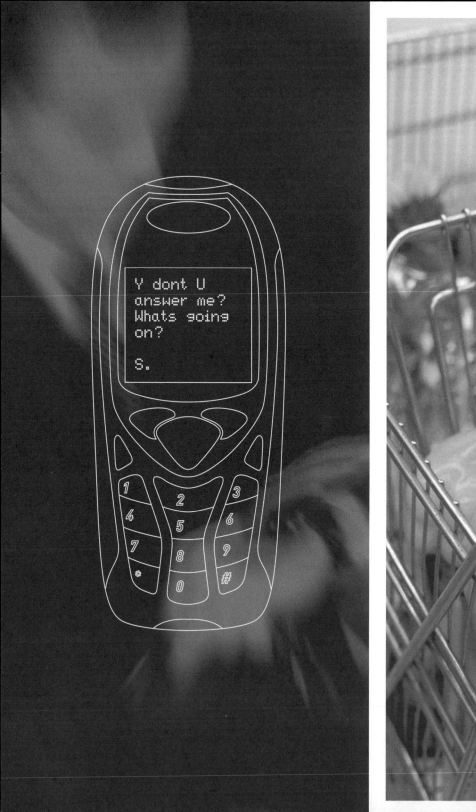

Hi Amelie!

Spring break is coming up and I need to get away from home for a while. You can imagine why, since our horrible mothers are sisters and so alike. Mine is getting on my nerves so much lately that all I do is plan my escape, day and night. That's how I came up with the idea of visiting you during spring break. Do you think they'll let me stay with you at the hotel?

I'll bring a mat and a sleeping bag. I'm ready to sleep on the floor just to get away from home. Please call soon and let me know if it's alright! Don't let me down!!! After all, the girls of our generation have got to stick together!

I'm begging you,

Sandra

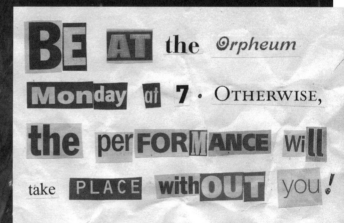

BE AT the *Orpheum* Monday at 7. OTHERWISE, the perFORMANCE will take PLACE withOUT you!

a friend

From: amarchand@webmail.bc
To: tim@yipee.ca
Subject: [no subject]

My wonderful blackmailer,
    It was a perfect evening. The show, the cafe, our time together afterwards, the way you held me so close... I had a great night.

    A.

Beautiful, gorgeous, exhilarating Amelie,
You forgot the incriminating
pictures! The proof of our hot date!
So that you'll always remember our
evening. Put the evidence on your mirror
or wherever else such things are kept.

Love,

Tim

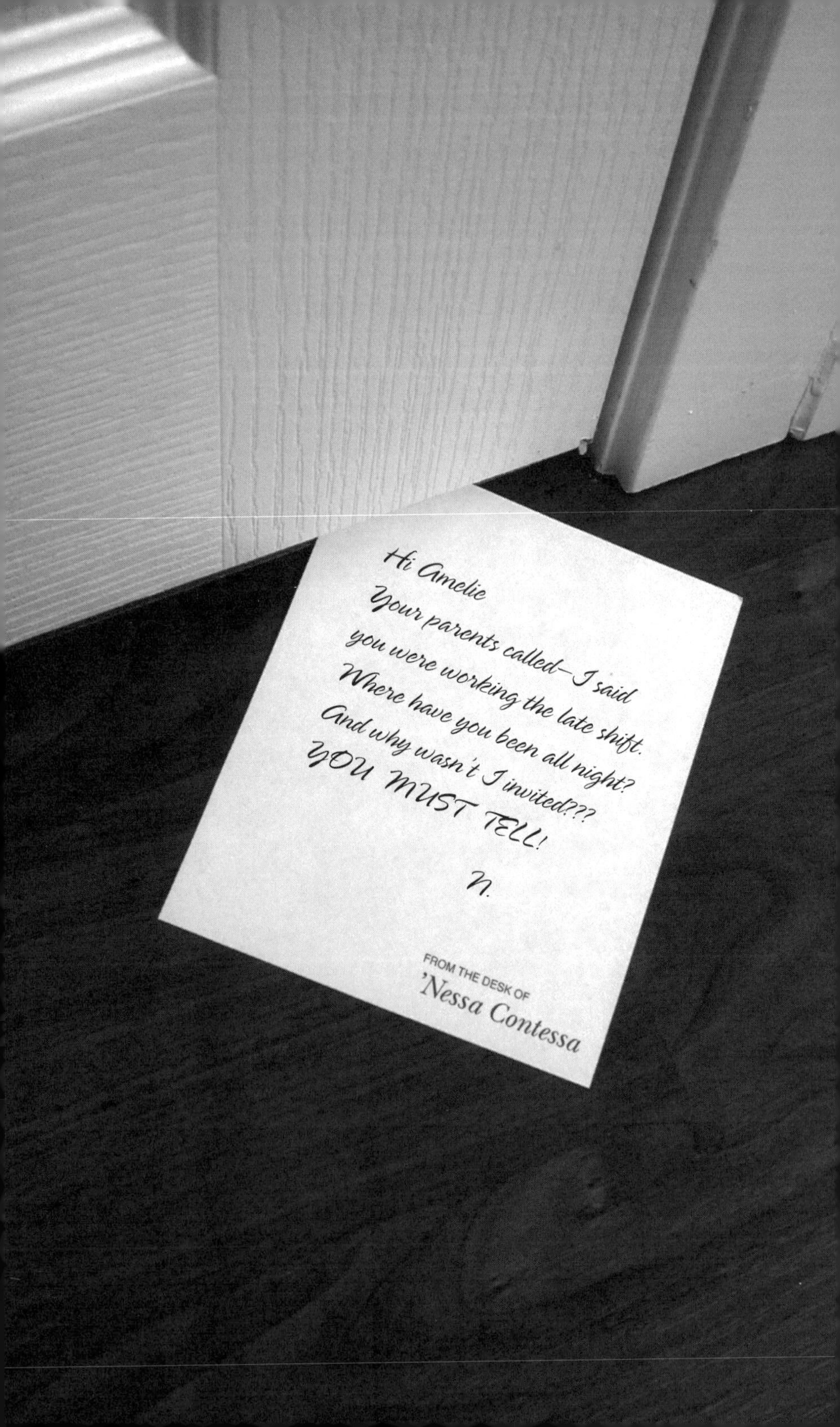
Hi Amelie
Your parents called—I said
you were working the late shift.
Where have you been all night?
And why wasn't I invited???
YOU MUST TELL!
N.
FROM THE DESK OF
'Nessa Contessa

Guest Check

Table No.	Server	Guests	Date

Meals	Amount

Amelie!
I'm so in love! I'm crazy about you! Now I understand what's meant by "I love you so much I could eat you up." That's how I feel. Waiter, please bring me an order of Amelie, hold the fries.

Sub-Total	
Tax	

Thank You!

TOTAL

081702

GA   Check #

Dear Mom,

Thank you so much for your understanding and support. I'm so glad you don't side with Sebastian. He imagines everything to be so easy: We get married, move to Chicago, and live happily ever after.

But for that kind of scenario he needs a chick from a B-movie, not me. I want to have a life of my own first, before I tie the knot. You really called it right when you said he confuses love with treating me like a child.

I'm sorry I had to cut our phone call short like that. I really didn't want to, but all of a sudden I felt like crying and I couldn't talk anymore.

I tried to call you back later, but Dad told me you were out playing bridge with your club and would be home late. I didn't want to talk to Dad about it—for him, Sebastian is like the son he never had. I'm sure he would have taken Sebastian's side—sometimes Dad is so old-fashioned.

I can't understand why Sebastian is making such a fuss. He's got me all confused. I guess that's why I'm writing you this letter. I'm trying to sort out my thoughts.

In the first place, I like Sebastian a lot. Whether he's the love of my life, I don't know. In the meantime, I've learned there is more than one way to love.

Also, I want to finish my management training. I don't want to give up my dreams to be a stay-at-home wife, dependent on her lord and master for better or for worse.

Whether I want to be a professional and have a career forever, I don't know right now. But either way, Sebastian should at least be able to accept the fact that I have work to do and don't want to quit my training.

Phew! Finally, it's all down. As much as I want Sebastian to understand, I'm sick at the thought that it might be over between him and me. I don't want to lose him.

Oh, Mom, I'm so confused. I want to be free and independent and at the same time be cuddled and cared for. Does that sound crazy?

You know what? I think I'm just going to go to bed now.

Good night.

Love,

Amelie

P.S. One more thing. But you're never ever allowed to use it against me, okay? Sometimes I just feel way too young to be thinking sooooo far into the future!

From: tim@yipee.ca
To: amarchand@webmail.bc
Subject: Missing you

Why don't you write? Why don't you call? Why is your cell off
all the time? Here I am sitting on the proverbial hot coals, because
all I want to do is run across town to your oh-so-fabulous hotel and
take you up in my arms. Instead, I'm stuck here, waiting for a sign
from you.
    GIVE ME A SIGN!!!

Tim

To my wonderful, beloved Amelie—

begging your forgiveness.
—S.

Omnitel C&IS
Suite 105
20500 Production Way   Tel   1+416 555 0465
Toronto, Ontario   Fax   1+416 555 6535
M3N 6T5 Canada   Web www.omnitelcis.com

omñitel COMMUNICATIONS & INFORMATION SYSTEMS

My beloved, enchanting Amelie,

With all my heart I'm asking your forgiveness!

I'm sending you this bouquet of your favorite yellow tulips, hoping you're no longer mad at me.

I've been way too brusque and way too demanding, and your reaction has been to turn away. And it hurts. A lot. I want you to understand that I didn't mean the things I said the way they must have sounded. All of a sudden, I was terribly afraid that you would call off our engagement plans, so I insisted on rights I naturally imagined I had, as your almost-fiancé.

Over the last two weeks, I've done some serious thinking. And I've realized something.

omntel COMMUNICATIONS & INFORMATION SYSTEMS

The most important thing is that I love you and that I want to live with you. Not only on my terms, but on yours as well. If you feel overwhelmed by my plans, then it's happened because of my naive assumption that everything was clear between us and already understood.

I now realize that my wishful thinking was the cause of our quarrel and that I surprised you with my suggestions. After battling my injured vanity and wounded pride, I can understand why you are keeping your distance.

It is one thing to have been together for two and a half years, and quite another to settle down for many years to come.

I would like us to be together. I would love to share an apartment with you, to watch you brush your teeth in the morning, to hear your breath at night. I want to watch you pick out clothes, eat spaghetti carbonara with you in bed. I want to cuddle up with you on the couch and watch videos and go shopping with you on Saturdays. I want to have fights with you about the dishes and paint the bathroom baby blue if we feel like it. I don't want to carry on with a weekend relationship where we don't share our day-to-day lives and have no idea what the other is going through. But now I've finally come to understand that you don't want that (yet).

I'll try to be patient. I'll try very hard and won't pressure you and won't push you. All I'll do is try to keep on being there for you.

I love you very much.

And miss you a lot.

Please forgive me (and return me to your good graces),

Love,

Bastian

Dear Sandra,

The good news is you can come.

The bad news is you can't stay with me at the hotel. It goes against my contract. But a co-worker of mine, Leah, lives in town and she said she's got a bed you can have (you can leave the mat at home). Hopefully we'll have lots of time together. At the moment I'm totally stressed out because we've got so many people on sick leave, but things can only get better. I'll call and clear it with your mom, okay?

See you soon,

Amelie

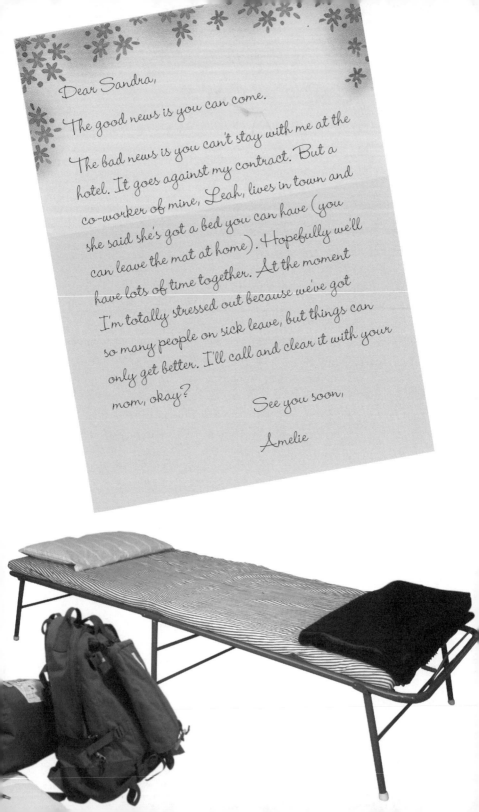

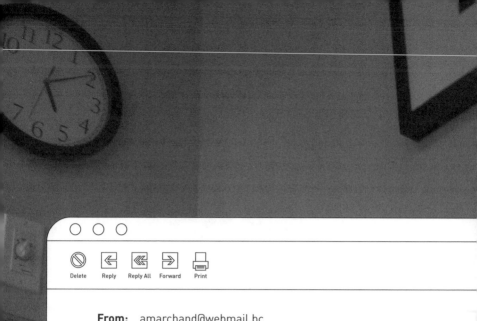

	From:	amarchand@webmail.bc
	To:	tim@yipee.ca
	Subject:	Sorry

Dear Tim,

   Please, please, don't be mad! I can't get away right now. In addition to my own shifts, I've got to fill in for a bunch of people who are sick. I'm not too well, myself. We'll talk soon, alright?

   Be patient.

   A.

Your cousin called.
She arrives tomorrow,
4 pm, at Vancouver airport.
You're supposed to pick her up.
OK?

Nessa

FROM THE DESK OF
'Nessa Contessa

From: amarchand@webmail.bc
To: tim@yipee.ca
Subject: Thanks

Dear, dear Tim,

You're a great help. Thank you so much. Sandra told me that you two are meeting up to hang out tomorrow. That's very sweet of you. I'm still crazy busy, but hopefully we'll see each other soon.

A little kiss on your left eye (so that you wink at me . . .),

Amelie ;-)

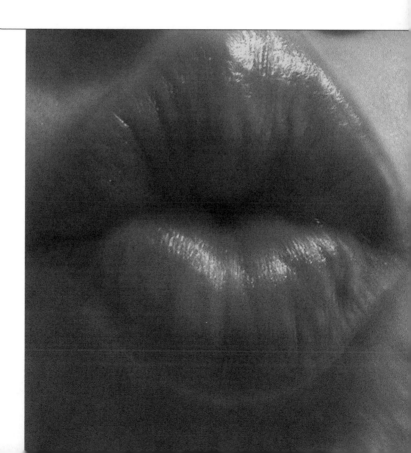

I'm sad, deathly sad.

One reason is because you're getting married. The other is because you kept quiet about it.

Sandra told me everything.

I've fallen head over heels in love with you, and you can't be bothered to be honest. Your lack of trust hurts me. Of course, what can a lowly high school student offer you—I must have been an amusing distraction while you picked out your wedding dress. Why did you pretend to love me while you were planning your life with someone else?

I never thought that hidden behind your beautiful face was someone so cold, so indifferent to the feelings of others. What was I for you? Your little boy toy?

I'm honestly sorry that I fell for you.

T.

ULTIMATE VANCOUVER

The Guide for the Low Budget. Where to Stay, Eat & Play.

Dear Ami,

I wanted to visit you at the hotel, but the people at reception told me that you were on duty in the restaurant and that I wasn't allowed to disturb you. Stupid rules. So i'm writing you this note to say i'm off to meet Tim again (he's soooo sweet). Why haven't you said anything about him before? You can leave a message on Leah's answering machine when you're allowed to mix with regular people again. Tim's an excellent tour guide.

XOXO
Sandra

...Guidebook for the starving traveller.

From: amarchand@webmail.bc
To: tim@yipee.ca
Subject: Sad

Tim,

That hurt.

I don't think I deserve that. I'm unhappy myself about everything that's happening.

Sebastian is not my fiancé, even though I always expected he would be. We've been going out for two years and now, without an official engagement or anything, he wants to get married and move to Chicago. But I don't know if that's what I want. Right now, I don't know anything.

The only thing I know is this: I had (and have?) a great time with you!

Please don't be mad at me, I can't take it!

I like you very, very much. You have to believe me. You were never an "amusing distraction"!

I'm at my wits' end and it doesn't help matters if I'm held up as the bad guy.

I didn't want this! I was afraid from the beginning to get involved with you. Be honest—you wouldn't let it go!

A.

P.S. The memory of what we've had together is very important to me. Please don't destroy it. And no, I don't have any regrets.

Steveston Seaquariu

"I like you very, very much." Thanks a lot. This coming from a girl who hates empty phrases. You might want to check this out—sounds like your kind of crowd.

Luckily, your cousin provides an attractive diversion . . .

More to See at the Seaquarium!

Special Exhibit:
Cold-Blooded Creatures of the Deep

Amelie—

Boss is angry that you didn't show. I'm heading down to cover your shift—said you are sick. Go to the doctor, get a note. I'll check on you later. Don't lose your head— you've only got one.

N.

FROM THE DESK OF
'Nessa Contessa

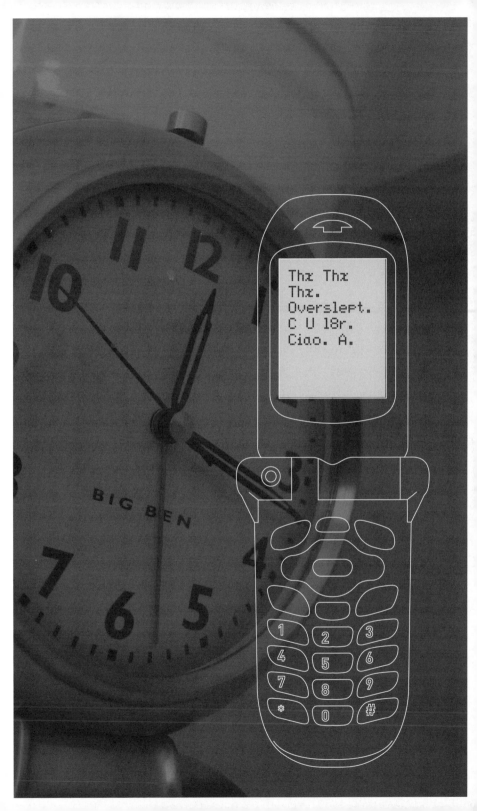

Dear Tim,

My favorite co-worker is covering for me this morning, so I can use this bit of quiet time to write to you. I guess there are a number of things that need to be cleared up.

Okay, you're right to complain about "I like you very, very much."

In order to be honest, it should have read "I fell in love with you." On one hand that's just great, but on the other hand it makes me helpless. I like Sebastian too (don't be mad, I'm trying to be totally truthful here), even though he's been putting lots of pressure on me lately. But he sees now that he was railroading me with his plans and he is trying to start over, and I'm impressed by his effort.

The way he's behaving now, I can see a future with him.

But for us, you and me, all I see are red roses and a series of midnight rendezvous. All very beautiful, but is that enough for us to build a relationship?

I have no idea.

I'm torn. And I feel tremendously helpless and stupid, being infatuated with two great guys at the same time and not knowing what to do next.

Okay, okay, not infatuated—in love.

Be honest—can you really see the two of us together long term?

I can already see you getting mad at me all over again, but my doubts are based more on our ambitions than on our difference in age. We are both at decisive points in our lives and could go in different directions. I plan to work abroad in the next two years. You, you don't have the faintest clue what you want to do next, whether university or something else. It won't work. In the end, it still might be a case of a fish not having any use for a bicycle (you and that silly cartoon!). I'm sure you're yelling now that we can make things work, and I would dearly love to believe that this fish could take part in the Tour de France, but fairy tales don't work in real life.

I care too much about you to lie to you. Try to be honest: even without Sebastian in the picture, would there truly be a future for us? Emotions alone are not enough, even if you don't want to hear that.

I don't like saying all these sensible, practical things. I find myself trying to be way too wise, acting way too mature and becoming way too pessimistic. I would prefer to be optimistic, hopeful, and crazy, to be totally off my rocker and completely in love—romantic, with pink flower dreams, cheesy music, and midnight meetings in the moonlight.

Instead, I have to try to be smart and sensible—and that has taken its toll so much that I've literally become sick.

Good-bye my friend of the funny letters.

I've got to end this one now because I'm about to break down and cry.

Love (even if you don't believe it),

Amelie

Delete   Reply   Reply All   Forward   Print

From: amarchand@webmail.bc
To: sebastian@hotpost.com
Subject: The weekend

Dear Bastian,

I'm coming home next weekend. We can talk about everything then.

I love you,

A.

120

The Royal Pacific Hotel
1518 Grand Avenue
Vancouver, B.C.
V1X 8G5 Canada

ROYAL PACIFIC HOTEL

Dear Leah,
Could you please tell Sandra that I have to cancel for this weekend? I need to go home. It's urgent. Besides, she's old enough that she'll have fun on her own. Tell her I'll drop her off at the airport on Tuesday.

Thank you,

Amelie

Hi crybaby,

Dry your tears and blow your nose with this.

In some ways, you're right, but in others, you're terribly wrong. Imagining that I will never see you again makes me feel so bad that I might start crying myself. But what would be the point, if I don't have you around to comfort me?

So, what did we have? A spring fling? With the summer coming, everything is over and done with?

If you want a future, I can make up some wild plans, too. How about a quaint little hotel in some nice college town where I do undergrad courses for medical school? You continue your management training and I set out to become a psychiatrist. And once your shift is over, I come and pick you up and we go for long walks in the moonlight, even when it's 20 below. And every night when we get home, I make you a big cup of hot cocoa—I make the world's best.

I love you, porter girl. Or is it just porter? (Okay, okay, head porter.)

I really hope you give us another chance.

Tim

P.S. Your cousin is quite NICE, but she's just not you.

Hi Amelie,

Thank you very much for this wonderful vacation, even if I saw so little of you.

Leah's mom was wonderful and your friend Tim took great care of me—thanks for letting me borrow him! I won't say anything about him at home. He mentioned rather sadly that he's afraid you might someday marry Sebastian. A mistake in my opinion. Tim is much more fun than that boring computer geek.

By the way, Leah has a very nice brother—did you know that? Marco might come and visit me in Calgary in the near future.

I would love to come back to Vancouver sometime. Maybe then we might see more of each other.

Ciao bella, molto grazie per tutto. (The result of two years of Italian lessons . . . sounds great, doesn't it?)

Ci vediamo,

Sandra

Hello little cousin,

I'm relieved that you don't hold all that's happened against me. The last two weeks have been nuts—thank you for being so understanding. Of course you're welcome to come back! And next time, we'll do tutto insieme— everything together. Capice?

A big bacio,
from Amelie

 Urban Everywhere.

| Delete | Reply | Reply All | Forward | Print |

From: nessacontessa@webmail.bc.
To: tim@yipee.ca
Subject: iced latte

Hi there,

Normally it's not my style to write notes to strangers. But while looking for a book in my friend Amelie's room, I discovered your name and e-mail address in a collection by my favorite poet. Since I'm terribly bored and Amelie went back home for the weekend, I thought I'd take the opportunity to chat with you about Leonard Cohen. And if you need the book back, I could even return it to you in person.

If you feel up to an iced latte, write me at nessacontessa@webmail.bc.

Vanessa

From: tim@yipee.ca
To: amarchand@webmail.bc
Subject: Vanessa

Dear, dear Amelie,

    We agreed on silence, but I need to ask you something. Did you set Vanessa on my tail? Does she know about me? I'm hoping that you're checking your e-mails, it's very, very urgent.

    Tim

From: amarchand@webmail.bc
To: tim@yipee.ca
Subject: Good luck

Oh, Tim,

I can't believe it... Vanessa tracked you down? No, rest assured, she doesn't know who you are. All she knows is that there is a "someone." If you met her somewhere, it's FATE.

I'm jealous, of course. If I remember your words correctly, she carries herself with such self-confidence, and that blonde hair...

Take care, my friend, my love.
See you sometime,
Amelie

Okay, okay, you said I shouldn't send you any messages. But I now declare that order only pertains to text messaging (over-abbreviated sweet talk), e-mails, and phone calls. After all, a letter is not a message.

I'm racking my brain, trying to think of a way I can convince you that we have this great chance to conquer life together. With your energy and my dedication, my fantasy and your common sense, your drive and my curiosity, and all our love combined, how can we fail? What other criteria do two people need to love each other FOREVER and NEVER be separated?

You're now saying, "One should never say never . . ." I can see you in front of me, trying not to smile, rolling your eyes. I kiss you, you don't say anything, and we just stand here looking into each other's eyes.

I'm not ready to give up!

Sebastian might have found you first, but now there's US and that's a reality you can't deny.

Tim

⊘	⬅	⬅⬅	➡	🖨
Delete	Reply	Reply All	Forward	Print

From: amarchand@webmail.bc
To: tim@yipee.ca
Subject: the future...

I arrive tomorrow at 6:55 p.m. Can you pick me up? I'm coming back to buy a crystal ball to see what my future holds. Maybe you know where I can get one?

Crystal balls
R exactly my
trade--clever
well-rounded
and
optimistic.